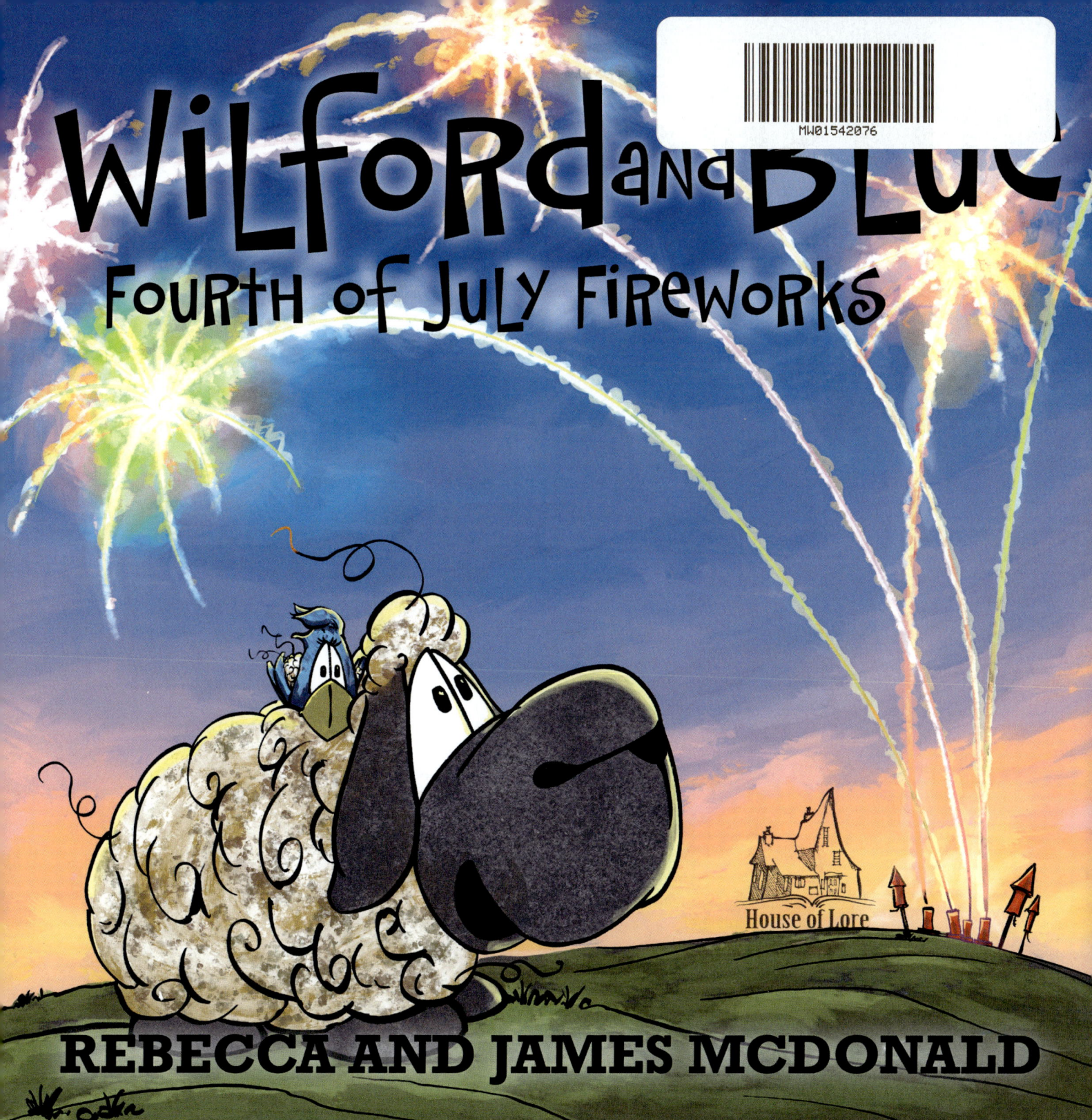

Wilford and Blue, Fourth of July Fireworks

Copyright © 2025 by Rebecca and James McDonald

ISBN: 978-1-950553-39-6

All rights reserved. No part of this publication may be reproduced, stored, or distributed in any form or by any means, electronic or mechanical, including photocopy, recording, or any information storage and retrieval system, without prior permission in writing from the publisher and copyright owner.

www.HouseOfLore.net

Check out these other titles from House of Lore

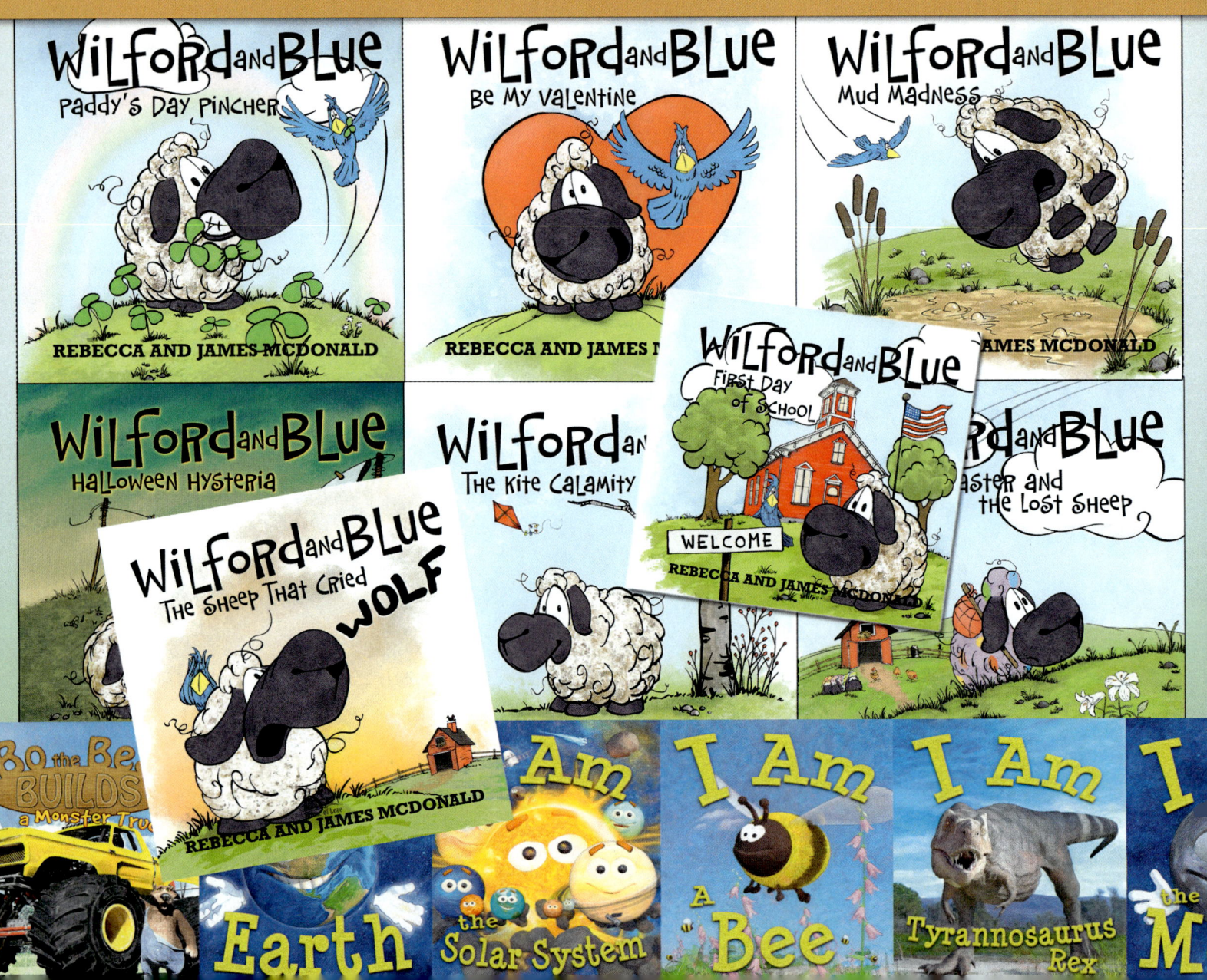

Made in the USA
Monee, IL
01 June 2025